PICTURE PUZZLES

Jenny Tyler
Illustrated and designed by
Graham Round

0 2250

Contents

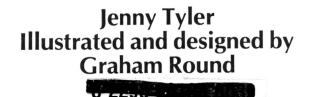

Hints on solving picture puzzles

To solve most of the puzzles in this book all you need do is use your powers of observation carefully. First of all, make sure you read the question properly so that you know what you are supposed to be looking for. Then look closely at each picture, or part of the picture if it is a big one, until you find it. Don't give up too soon – you will often find things in the pictures that you didn't see at all when you first looked.

For the "spot the difference" kind of puzzle, look at part of one of the pictures and try to fix an image of it in your mind. Then look at the same part of the other picture and compare it with the picture in your mind.

There is a picture symbol, like this:

next to some of the puzzles. This means that a pencil and paper would be useful. For mazes, it is best to lay tracing paper over the top and follow the way through with a coloured pencil. If you make a mistake, you can throw the paper away and start again with a new piece.

For a few of the puzzles there is a clue on page 32. These have a picture symbol like this:

next to them. You will find the answers to all these picture puzzles on pages 26 to 32.

Cardboard train

This collection of boxes, rolls and corks was used to make a model of a train. Every single piece was used but nothing extra was added. Which of these models is the one that was built from this group of objects?

A

B

C

Match pictures and badges

Here are some boxes of pictures and some badges. What you have to do is find the badge which best fits the *group* of pictures in each box.

First choose a badge for the group of pictures in the BLUE box.

Next choose a badge for the group of things in the RED box.

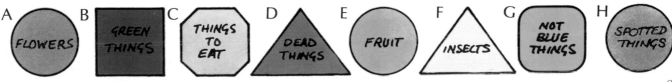

A FLOWERS

B GREEN THINGS

C THINGS TO EAT

D DEAD THINGS

E FRUIT

F INSECTS

G NOT BLUE THINGS

H SPOTTED THINGS

Jigsaw pieces

Here are six jigsaw pieces which will fit together if you put them in the right order. Which piece goes next to which?

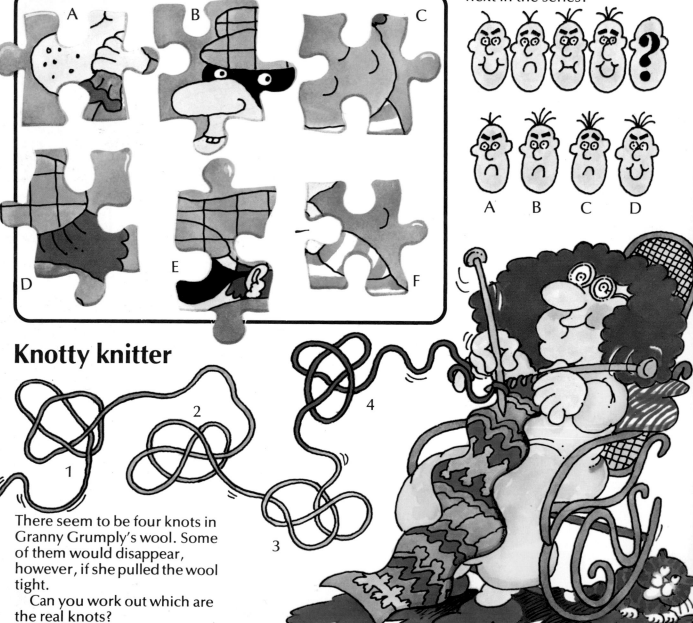

Which face is next?

Here is a series of faces. Can you work out which of the faces in the row below should come next in the series?

Knotty knitter

There seem to be four knots in Granny Grumply's wool. Some of them would disappear, however, if she pulled the wool tight.

Can you work out which are the real knots?

4

Which map?

Curly, Carrots, Fingers and Joe each tried to draw a map of where they live. Only one of them got the map right. Who was it?

CARROTS

JOE

FINGERS

CURLY

Tangled lines

Four inexperienced anglers went fishing together. Find out what each of them has caught.

1   2   3   4

Mirror puzzle

Countess Crinklyface is putting on her make-up. Which of the four pictures below shows her face as she sees it in the mirror?

A

B

C

D

Fake picture

The owner of this picture claims that it was painted over 300 years ago. But famous art historian, Art Y. Brush, says it is a fake because it is full of mistakes. How many mistakes can you find?

If you get stuck, look at the clue on page 32.

Three cats

Which of these cats is the biggest? Guess first, then measure to see if you were right.

6

Mixed-up snapshots

Sammy cut his holiday snapshots into pieces and mixed them up. His Granny soon worked out which piece belonged to which snapshot. Can you?

Find the twin cats

Two of these cats are the same. The others are slightly different in some way. Can you find the twins?

8

Caught red-handed

Trapped in a beam of light, Light-fingered Pete is caught in the act of stealing the jewels. But there is something wrong with this picture. Can you work out what it is?

Easy chair

This chair was drawn in one continuous line, without the pen being removed from the page and without any part of the line being covered twice. Can you work out how?

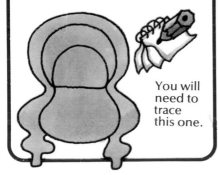

You will need to trace this one.

Doodlesaur puzzle

Here are some Doodlesaurs.

Here are some creatures which are not Doodlesaurs.

Which of these creatures are Doodlesaurs?

1

2

3

4

9

What does the letter say?

This torn-up letter was found in a waste-paper basket.
  Can you work out what it says?

Which cat comes next?

Which one of the cats numbered 1 to 4 below should come next in the row on top of the wall?

1   2   3   4

Dice problem

Which of the dice below could be made from this unfolded one?

A   B   C   D

10

Mixed-up puppet

Can you sort out this puppet's strings?

A B C D E F G H

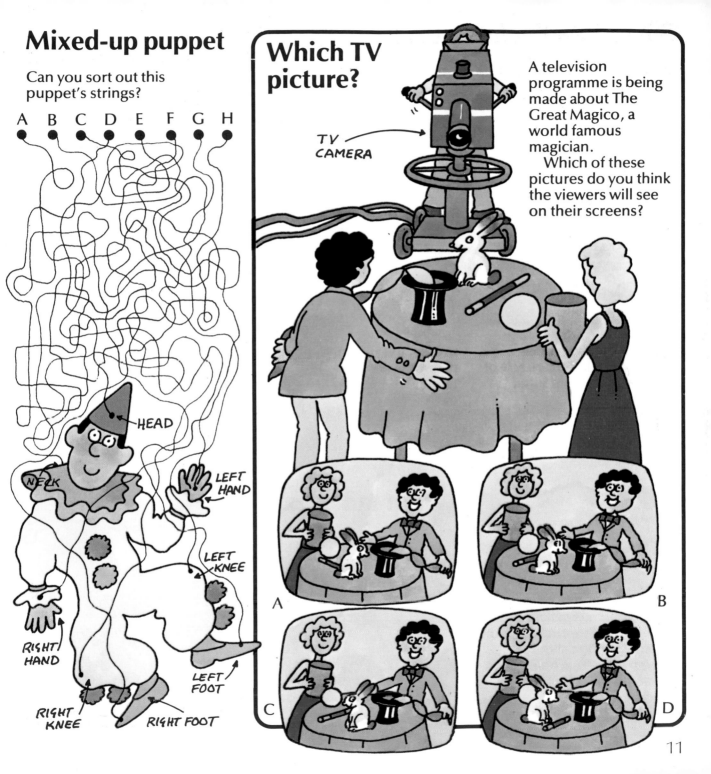

HEAD

NECK

LEFT HAND

LEFT KNEE

RIGHT HAND

RIGHT KNEE

RIGHT FOOT

LEFT FOOT

Which TV picture?

TV CAMERA

A television programme is being made about The Great Magico, a world famous magician.

Which of these pictures do you think the viewers will see on their screens?

A

B

C

D

Slug puzzle

Two umbrellas

One day, the gardener found seven slugs in the lettuce patch. He quickly put a circle of slug repellent round some of them.

Look at this rainy day picture. Whose umbrella has the longest handle? (Guess first, then measure to see if you were right.)

MR. THIN

MRS. FAT

Trick question

This clever acrobatic lady can do two tricks. First she puts a pole between her teeth and balances a ball on each end.

Next she balances a pole and a ball on her chin.

Do you think she uses the same pole for both tricks? (Guess first.)

He has enough repellent left to make two more circles of the same size. Where should he put them so that each slug is cut off from all the others?

If you get stuck, there is a clue on page 32.

Rabbit tail puzzle

FLUFF

Do you think that it is further from Hoppy's tail to Fluff's than from Fluff's tail to Big Ears'? (Measure to see if you guessed right.)

BIG EARS

HOPPY

12

Party puzzle

Which of the six tables on the right is laid exactly like the one at the party mentioned below? Read the following information and work it out.

Jim said there was a big cake with pink icing and six chocolate drops on top. There was a plate of square sandwiches too. The table was covered with a red striped cloth.

Fred said there were triangular sandwiches. Next to these, on the right, there was a large red jelly.

Joan said the jelly was green and there were square chocolate biscuits.

Sue said she specially liked the little cakes with cherries on top. There were six of those. She thought the tablecloth had yellow spots on it.

Jack said the cake was covered with white icing. There were no chocolate biscuits and the sandwiches were horrible.

Jack later admitted that he had not told the truth and Joan said she had got confused with another party. The other three were right.

Mirror pictures

If you rest the edge of a mirror in a certain place on some pictures, you will see that the reflection in the mirror completes the picture, like this:

The place where you rest the mirror when this happens is called a "line of symmetry". Look at the pictures and work out (using a mirror if you like) which ones have a line of symmetry.

Time puzzle

These pictures show scenes from long ago. Can you sort them out into the order in which they happened?

Find the missing pieces

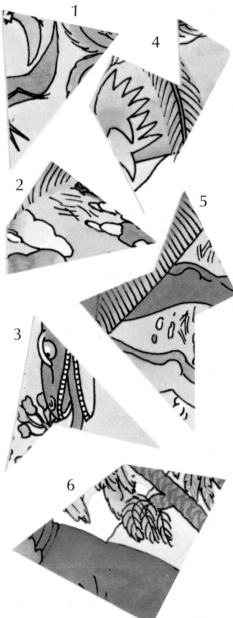

These pieces belong to the picture on the left. Which piece fits where?

1

2

3

4

5

6

A

B

C

D

E

F

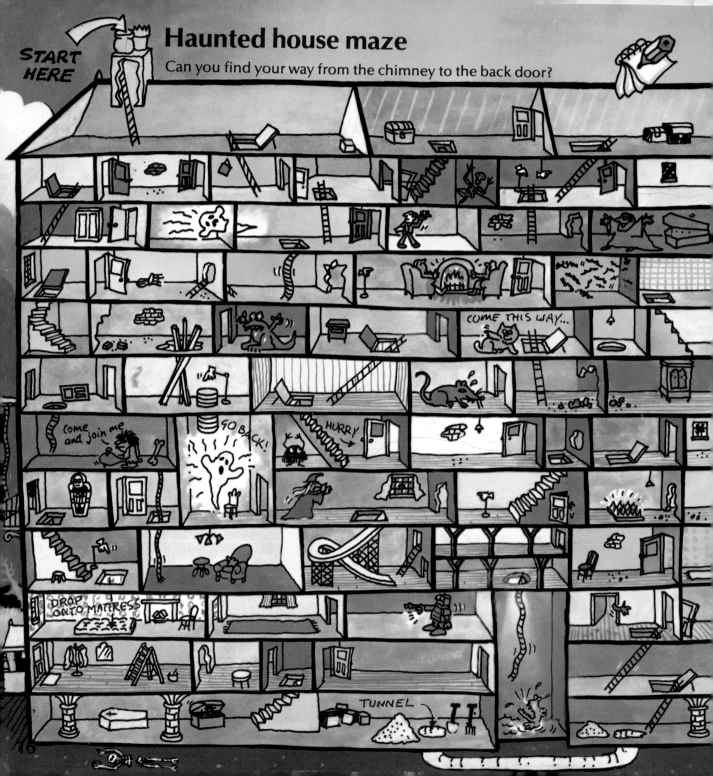

Haunted house maze

Can you find your way from the chimney to the back door?

17

How many hiding places?

These two old ladies are really spies in disguise, but they quickly hid all their equipment when they heard you coming. Can you find all the places where they have hidden things?

Tangled group

Can you sort out whose guitar is plugged into each amplifier?

STRUMMER (RHYTHM GUITAR)

RED (BASS GUITAR)

SPIDER (LEAD GUITAR)

PINKIE (SECOND LEAD GUITAR)

A   B   C   D

Picture pairs

Each of these coloured shapes has something special in common with one of the others. Sort them out into twos and say what each pair has in common.

Odd picture

Which of these pictures is the odd one out and why?

19

Label the bag

Which of these labels best describes the contents of the bag at the bottom of the page?

A — Paper things

B — Red and blue things

C — Not round things

D — Not green things

E — Things to read

F — Things to eat

Spot the difference

These two pictures look the same at first sight, but when you look closely you will find that some things are different. There are, in fact, 20 differences between the pictures. See if you can find them all.

Which cog?

Sue needed a new cog wheel for her bicycle. She knew it must have ten square teeth and a round hole in the centre. The man in the shop told her to sort through this box. Which one should she buy?

21

Where is the missing painting?

There has been a robbery at the Abstract Art Gallery. The Gallery officials are particularly upset because the painting was part of a famous and valuable sequence. The police have come to solve the crime, but unfortunately no-one at the Gallery can remember exactly what the painting looks like.

Can you tell them which of the paintings below is the stolen one?

If you get stuck, look up the clue on page 32.

1

2

3

4

Another odd picture

Which of these pictures is the odd one out and why?

A

B

C

D

E

Which house fits the plan?

This is a plan of the ground floor of a house. Can you work out which of these houses it belongs to?

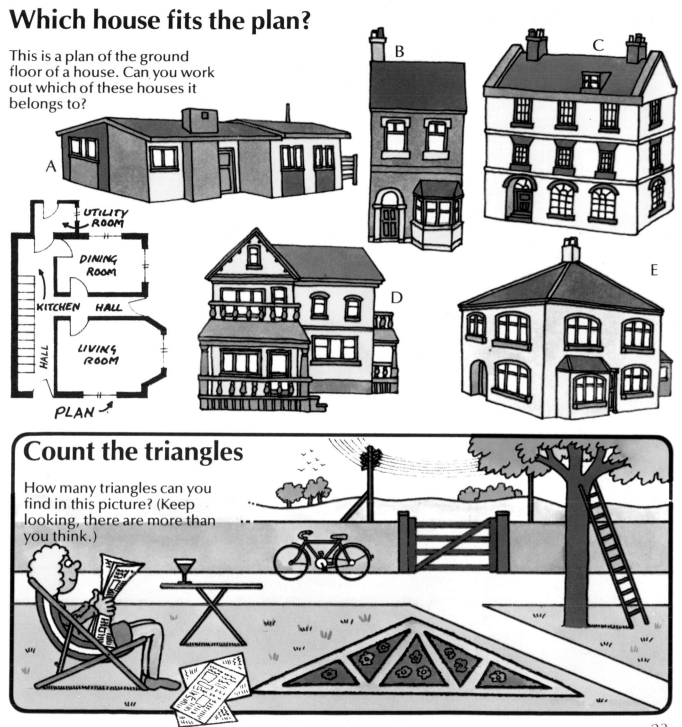

Count the triangles

How many triangles can you find in this picture? (Keep looking, there are more than you think.)

Find the mistakes

There are 23 things wrong with this picture. Can you find out what they all are?

BATH
YOUR
BABY...

...WITH
BLOGGS
CAR SHINE

AUDIO-VISUAL

FRUITERER

SPECIAL
OFFER

TOYSHOP

CAFÉ TEAS

Find the odd shoe

These shoes all look the same, but one is slightly different from the others. Which one?

If you get stuck,
there is a clue on page 32.

A B C D E F G H

Identibits puzzle

Which of these "identibits" belong to the face shown here?

Mixed-up story

This picture-strip story is all mixed up. Sort out the pictures and put them in the order in which they could have happened.

If you get stuck, look at the clue on page 32.

25

Answers

Page 3

Cardboard train

Model A was built from the collection of objects in the picture.

Match pictures and badges

GREEN THINGS is best for the blue box.

NOT BLUE THINGS is the best badge for the red box.

Page 4

Jigsaw pieces

Here is the completed jigsaw.

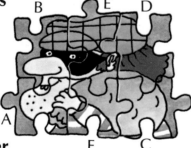

Knotty knitter

Knots 1 and 3 are real.

Which face is next?

Face B should come next in the row.

Page 5

Which map?

Fingers was the only one to draw the right map.

Tangled lines

Fisherman 1 caught nothing.
Fisherman 2 caught the box of treasure.
Fisherman 3 caught the wheel.
Fisherman 4 caught the fish.

Page 6

Mirror puzzle

Picture C shows what Countess Crinklyface sees in the mirror.

Three cats   They are all the same size.

Fake picture

There are 22 mistakes. Here they all are:

Page 8

Mixed-up snapshots

Here are the sorted out pictures.

Find the twin cats

Cats 2 and 6 are the twins.

Page 9

Caught red-handed

The shadow of Light-fingered Pete is pointing in the wrong direction – it should be pointing into the picture.

Easy chair

Follow the arrows on this picture to see how to draw the chair.

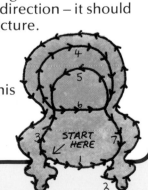

Doodlesaur puzzle

Creatures 2 and 4 are Doodlesaurs, 1 and 3 are not. Here is how you can tell:
The first three pictures tell you that Doodlesaurs have red eyes, straight tails, sometimes have spots and are blue or green.

Page 10

What does the letter say?

Here is the complete letter, so you can read what it says.

Which cat comes next?

Cat 4 should come next on the wall.

Dice puzzle

Dice A and D are the same as the unfolded one.

Page 11

Mixed-up puppet

String A goes to the puppet's head.
String B goes to the puppet's right hand.
String C goes to the puppet's left foot.
String D goes to the puppet's left knee.
String E goes to the puppet's left hand.
String F goes to the puppet's neck.
String G goes to the puppet's right foot.
String H goes to the puppet's right knee.

Which TV picture?

Picture B is the one the viewers will see.

Page 12

Slug puzzle

The picture above shows where the slug repellent circles should go.

Two umbrellas

Mr Thin's umbrella handle is the same length as Mrs Fat's.

Trick question

She can do both tricks with the same pole because it is the same length in both pictures.

Rabbit tail puzzle

The distance from Hoppy's tail to Fluff's is the same as that from Fluff's to Big Ears'.

Page 13

Party puzzle

Table 4 shows what there was to eat at the party.

Page 14

Mirror pictures

Pictures 1, 3, 4, 6 and 8 have a line of symmetry.

Time puzzle

The correct order for the pictures is:
4 (Dinosaur, which lived about 100 million years ago)
3 (Stone Age hunters, who lived about 1½ million years ago)
7 (Ancient Egyptian pharaoh, about 3½ thousand years ago)
2 (Ancient Roman soldier, who lived about 2,000 years ago)
1 (Medieval knight, who lived about 900 years ago)
8 (Elizabethan man, who lived about 400 years ago)
5 (Penny-farthing bicycle, which was in use about 100 years ago)
6 (Early aeroplane, in use about 60 years ago)

Page 15

Find the missing pieces

The pieces fit as follows:
piece 1 (B), piece 2 (E), piece 3 (A), piece 4 (D), piece 5 (F), piece 6 (C).

Page 16 Haunted house maze   Here is the route through the house.

Page 18

How many hiding places?

◀ The hiding places are ringed on the picture on the left. There are 21 of them altogether.

Page 19

Tangled group

Pinkie's guitar is plugged into D.
Spider's guitar is plugged into A.
Red's guitar is plugged into B.
Strummer's guitar is plugged into C.

Picture pairs

1 and 8 are a pair because they both have spots.
2 and 4 are a pair because they are both the same shape.

6 and 5 are a pair because they both have stripes.
3 and 7 are a pair because they are both the same colour.

Odd picture

Picture 4 is the odd one. it is the only back view. All the others show front views.

Page 20

Label the bag

Label D fits the bag best.

Spot the differences

The places where the two pictures are different are ringed in this picture. ▶

Page 21

Which cog?

Sue should buy cog 5.

Page 22

Where is the missing painting?

Picture 2 is the stolen one.

Another odd picture

Picture C is the odd one out – it is the only thing in the group which doesn't come in pairs.

Page 23

Which house fits the plan?

House E is the only one which fits.

Count the triangles

There are at least 31 triangles in the picture. You can see where they are on this picture. You may be able to find some more but remember they must be complete triangles.

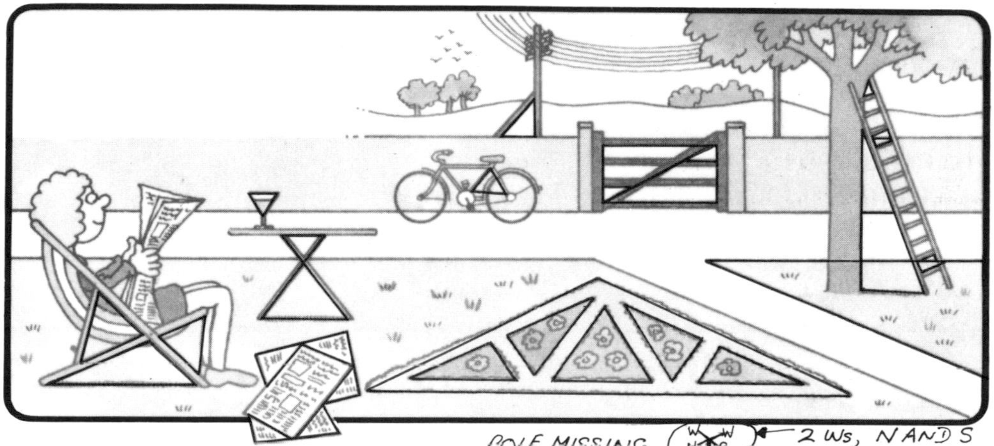

Page 24

Find the mistakes

The wrong things are ringed in this picture.

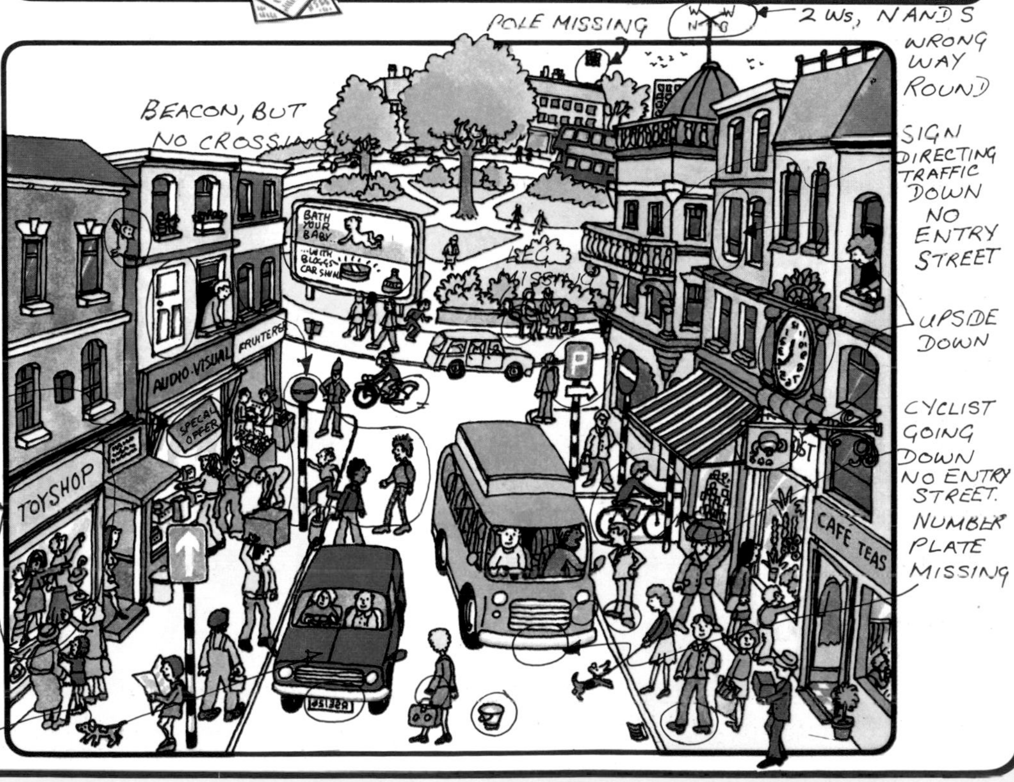

POLE MISSING
2 WS, N AND S WRONG WAY ROUND
BEACON, BUT NO CROSSING
SIGN DIRECTING TRAFFIC DOWN NO ENTRY STREET
LEG MISSING
UPSIDE DOWN
SPELLING ERROR
CYCLIST GOING DOWN NO ENTRY STREET.
NUMBER PLATE MISSING
WRONG SHOP SIGN
TRAFFIC GOING WRONG WAY ALONG ONE-WAY STREET.
BATH YOUR BABY..
TOYSHOP
AUDIO-VISUAL
SPECIAL OFFER
CAFÉ TEAS

Find the odd shoe

Shoe F is the different one.

Page 25

Identibits puzzle

Pieces 2, 3, 4, 6, 9, 10 and 14 fit the face, the others don't.

Mixed-up story

The pictures should be in this order; 4, 2, 5, 1, 3.

Clues

Page 6

Fake picture

There are 22 things wrong. See if you can find them all before looking at the answer.

Page 12

Slug puzzle

The picture shows where the second circle goes. Now see if you can work out the position of the third one.

Page 22

Where is the missing painting?

Notice that the picture is turned round each time and that the colours move round too, but always stay in the same order. Now have another look.

Page 24

Find the odd shoe

Look very very carefully at the laces.

Page 25

Mixed-up story

Notice how dirty the players are.

NUMBER PUZZLES

Contents

Hints on solving number puzzles

All the puzzles in this book are based on simple arithmetic, so you don't have to be a maths expert to solve them. All you need to know about is adding, subtracting, multiplying, dividing and easy fractions.

When you are doing the puzzles, always read the question carefully and look out for catches. Some of them sound more difficult than they really are. Take your time too – it doesn't matter how long it takes you to work out the answers.

It is a good idea to have some paper handy for doing sums on. You are less likely to make mistakes than if you do the calculations in your head. There is a picture symbol like this:

next to the puzzles for which you are most likely to need to write things down.

You will find some of the puzzles easier than others. If you come across one that seems too difficult, leave it and move on to another. It may seem easier when you come back to it another time. You will find a picture symbol, like this:

at the end of some of the puzzles. This means there is a clue on page 64 which will help you solve the puzzle without giving you the answer.

You will find all the answers on pages 58 to 63.

Can you do Martian maths?

Martian numbers are often written differently from Earth numbers. For instance, Earth number 481 is written

in Martian numbers. Also

in Martian numbers is the same as 2963 in Earth numbers.

Can you work out what

is in Earth numbers?

Can you also work out what

is?

You should now know the Martian equivalents of all the Earth numbers from 0 to 9. See if you can use them to help Marty Martian with his homework. Give the answers in Martian numbers (for Marty) and in Earth numbers.

Marty's maths homework

a) What is $\frac{1}{\odot}$ of ☺☺ ?

b) Melissa Martian gives $\frac{1}{\odot}$ of the Martian coins in her pocket to her friend. She started with ☺☺ coins. How many did she have left?

c) If it takes ☺ day for ☺ men to dig ☺ hole, how long will it take them to dig ☺ holes?

d) Minnie, Mel and Miranda's ages added together come to ☺☺. Minnie is ☺. Mel is ☺. How old is Miranda?

If you get stuck, look at the clue on page 64.

35

Ancient sum puzzle

This ancient clay tablet was dug up in the desert. The experts who are trying to deciper it have worked out that:

⇨ is =.

△ is 1.

□ is 5.

□/△ is 7.

Can you work out what is on the tablet?

If you get stuck, look at the clue on page 64.

Next number 1

Here are some members of Johnny's Gym Club. The numbers on their shirts form a series. Can you work out which number the end person should have on the front of his shirt?

3   8   15   24   ?

Next number 2

Now work out what number he should have on the back of his shirt.

3   2   4   3   ?

What colour?

If all odd numbers are red and all even numbers are blue, what colour is an odd number plus an even number?

How many chocolates?

Penny's big brother is trying to get a share of her big box of birthday chocolates.

"Put some in my pockets," he said. "One in the first pocket, two in the second, four in the third, and so on – doubling the number for each pocket."

"I have four pockets in my jeans and three in my jacket."

How many chocolates was he expecting Penny to give him?

Number boxes

Each of these boxes contains a set of numbers. Can you work out what the set is and find another number to go in each box?

A   B

Cubes

This wooden building brick is patterned all over, and each of its sides measures 20cm. Imagine it is sawn into smaller cubes with 10cm sides.

How many of the small cubes will have some pattern on them?

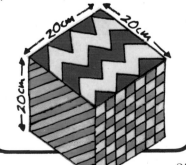

Clare's cousins

This is a picture of Clare with some of her family and friends.

Clare's grandmother on her father's side had two children, who each had two children.

Her grandmother on her mother's side also had two children. They, too, each had two children.

Can you work out how many cousins Clare has?

Tennis game puzzle

Jo, Sue, Sam and Liz decided to hold a tennis tournament. They all had to play each other once. They were quite surprised to find how long it took to play the tournament. How many matches were played altogether?

Look for a clue on page 64 if you get stuck.

Chocolate puzzle

Can you work out how many 75g chocolate bars there are in a dozen?

Bicycle wheel sum

How many spaces are there between the spokes of two eight-spoked bicycle wheels?

Pie puzzle

Uncle Dan is cutting one of his famous big pies into slices – one large one for himself and several smaller ones for the rest of the family.

When he has finished, three-quarters of the number of slices to the left of the big slice will be six.

How many slices will there be altogether?

If you get stuck, you will find a clue on page 64.

How many squares?

How many squares can you find in the pattern on this carpet?

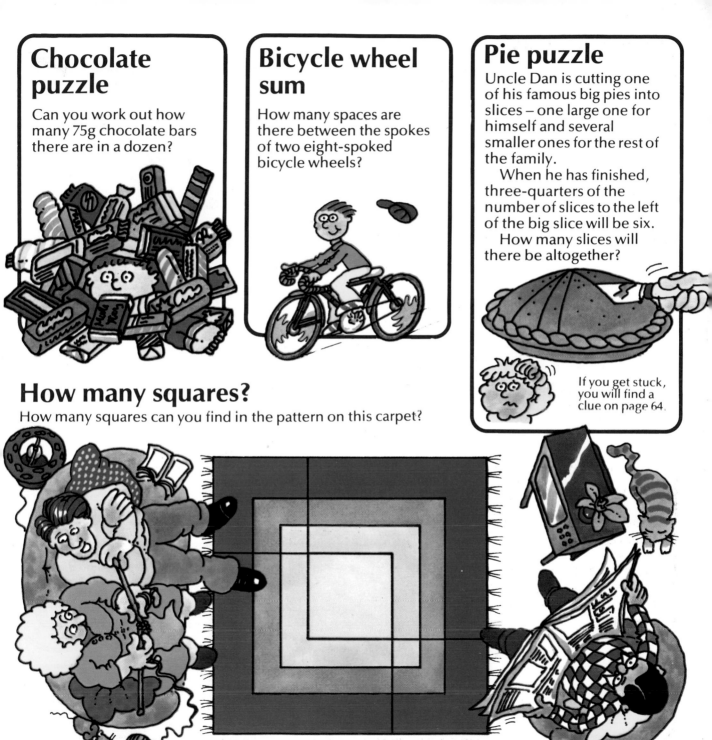

39

Which button?

The intrepid explorer, Space Ace, has been trapped in a room with a time bomb by the aliens. He has 7.38 minutes to work out which button opens the door.

He knows that the buttons are numbered from 1 to 16, with no number appearing twice. He also knows that the numbers in each row, column and diagonal add up to 34.

To open the door, he must press button number 1. All other buttons will trigger off the bomb.

Which button should he press to get out safely?

Watch face sum

Can you put one straight line across this watch face so that the numbers in each of the two parts add up to the same number? One of the four pictures on the right gives the correct answer.

A   B   C   D

Magic numbers

THINK OF A NUMBER AND THEN DO THE FOLLOWING THINGS TO IT.

TAKE AWAY 2

MULTIPLY THE RESULT BY 3

ADD 12

DIVIDE THE RESULT BY 3

ADD 5

TAKE AWAY THE NUMBER YOU FIRST THOUGHT OF.

We have written the answer on page 59. Look it up and see if we are right.

Now try again with another number.

Quick question

What is half of two divided by a half?

Lamp post puzzle

The lamp posts in Pete and Dave's street are evenly spaced. The first one stands right on the corner and the third one is next to Pete's front gate. Dave's front gate is next to the sixth lamp post.

How many times further down the street does Dave have to walk than Pete to get from corner to his front gate?

Martian cake puzzle

How much did it cost Marty Martian's Mum to bake a cake from the recipe below? You can see how much things cost on Mars from this price list from a local supermarket. Martian money, incidentally, is called Moons and Dragons – 50 Moons make 1 Dragon.

MARTIAN CAKE RECIPE

Mix up the following in a big bowl:

- 500g green flour
- 100g nut dust
- 100g space butter
- 250ml sweet juice
- 2 marsbird eggs

bake for 1 hour in a hot marsgas oven.

SUPERMARS SUPERMARKET
— PRICELIST —

Green flour   2 Dragons for 1 kilo

Nut dust (best quality) 500g for 3 Dragons

Space butter   2 Dragons 20 Moons for 1 kilo

Sweet juice (special offer) 40 Moons a litre

Marsbird eggs 1 Dragon for 10

Cylinders of Marsgas (economy size, lasts 100hrs) 10 Dragons each

Model train puzzle

The biggest model shop in town has an enormous model railway layout with a metre-long tunnel.

The shop assistant says that the train is also a metre long and is travelling at 60 metres a minute as it enters the tunnel.

How long does it take for the train to pass completely through the tunnel?

New numbers

If

is 358

and

is 106,

what is this?

What is the answer, in new number writing, if you add this

to the previous number?

Washing day puzzle

If it takes 45 minutes for one wet shirt to dry on the washing line, how long does it take three shirts to dry?

Football shirt numbers

Northend United soccer club has enough players for two teams with six reserves for each team. Their shirts are numbered, on the front only, from one to 34.

How many figure 1's are needed for their new set of shirts?

The odd number

Which of these numbers is the odd one out?

18

75

39

47

51

Car parking puzzle

Three cars are about to park in the remaining three spaces in this car park. How many different colour combinations can they make by parking in these spaces?

This car doesn't move.

How heavy is the cat?

Look at these pictures. Can you
work out how much the cat
weighs by itself (in grammes)?

1

EACH JAR
OF JAM
WEIGHS
500 G

SCALES ARE
EXACTLY BALANCED

2

SAME
SCALES
ALSO
EXACTLY
BALANCED

Calendar counting

How many months
have 30 days?

How many people?

Have you any idea how
many people lying head to
toe are needed to stretch
right round the Earth? Is
the number closest to:
a) 30 million
b) 1 million
or c) 100 million?

45

Garden path puzzle

These snails started out from the opposite edges of the garden path at the same time. They both moved at exactly the same speed. When they met, they were 50cm from the right-hand edge of the path.

Can you work out how wide the path is?

Hungry bookworm

This Large Boring Book is 10cm thick. It has 3,000 pages in it and its covers are made of board which is ½cm thick.

How many centimetres through the book must the worm eat in order to reach page number 1000?

LARGE BORING BOOK

Liquorice sticks

Spotty bought ten sticks of liquorice and ate all but four. How many did she have left to share with her friend.

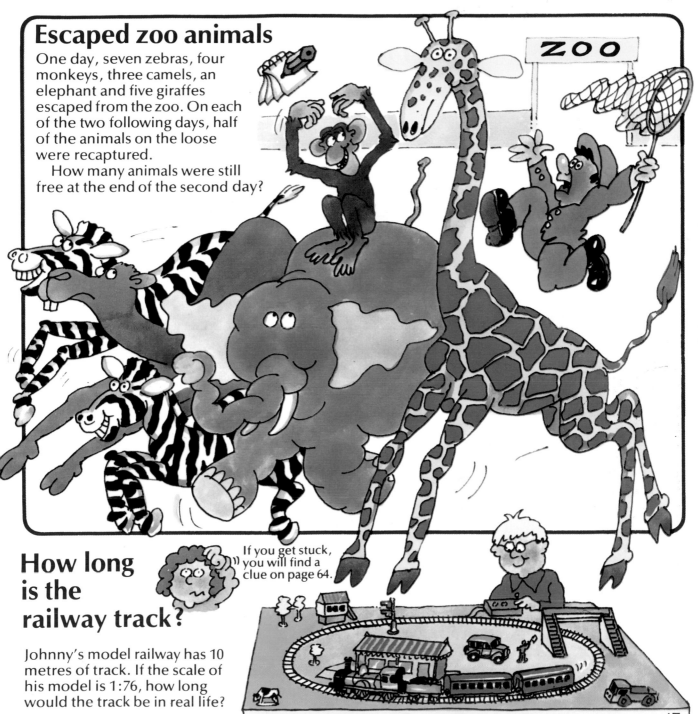

Escaped zoo animals

One day, seven zebras, four monkeys, three camels, an elephant and five giraffes escaped from the zoo. On each of the two following days, half of the animals on the loose were recaptured.

How many animals were still free at the end of the second day?

ZOO

If you get stuck, you will find a clue on page 64.

How long is the railway track?

Johnny's model railway has 10 metres of track. If the scale of his model is 1:76, how long would the track be in real life?

47

Mystery tour

Freddie's school's annual outing was to be a mystery tour – even the driver didn't know where they were going. To find the route, he was given this map. Every time he came to a road junction, he had to solve a riddle and drive in the direction indicated by the correct answer.

Can you work out where Freddie and his friends ended up?

Twice five plus the wings of a bird.

The legs of a dog plus a soccer team.

The days of April divided by the sides of a triangle.

Half the letters in the alphabet.

Half the days in a leap year minus the toes on one foot.

The hours in three days.

The grammes in a kilogramme minus the colours in a rainbow.

The legs of a centipede minus the millimetres in a centimetre.

The heels of 27 pairs of socks.

Fairground

Circus

Nature walk

Theatre

12 14 10 8

11 13 26

11 8

10

7 15 11

177 361 15

178 173

36

76 72

900 0

9 90

990

1007

600 993

7 700

54 27 108

2

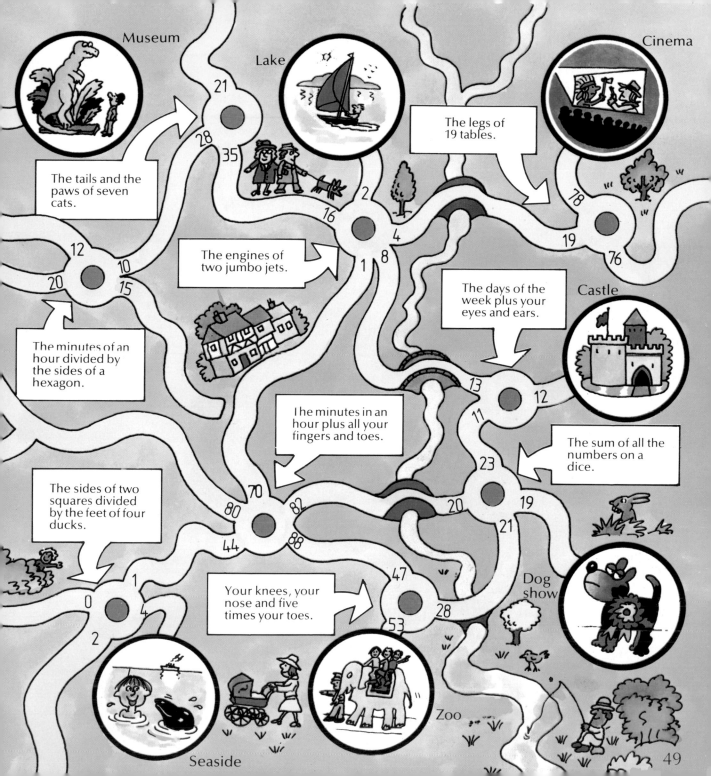

Museum

Lake

Cinema

21

28

35

The legs of
19 tables.

The tails and the
paws of seven
cats.

12

10

20

15

2

16

4

1   8

The engines of
two jumbo jets.

78

19

76

Castle

The days of the
week plus your
eyes and ears.

The minutes of an
hour divided by
the sides of a
hexagon.

The minutes in an
hour plus all your
fingers and toes.

13

12

11

The sum of all the
numbers on a
dice.

23

The sides of two
squares divided
by the feet of four
ducks.

70

80   82

20   19

21

44   88

Dog
show

1

0

4

Your knees, your
nose and five
times your toes.

47

28

2

53

Zoo

Seaside

49

Park puzzle

This picture shows a busy afternoon in the park. It doesn't look very busy, though, because all the people are invisible.

Can you work out how many people there are in the park?

Block and box puzzle

How many ways could you put the alphabet block shown here into this red wooden box?

If you get stuck, there is a clue on page 64.

If you get stuck, there is a clue on page 64.

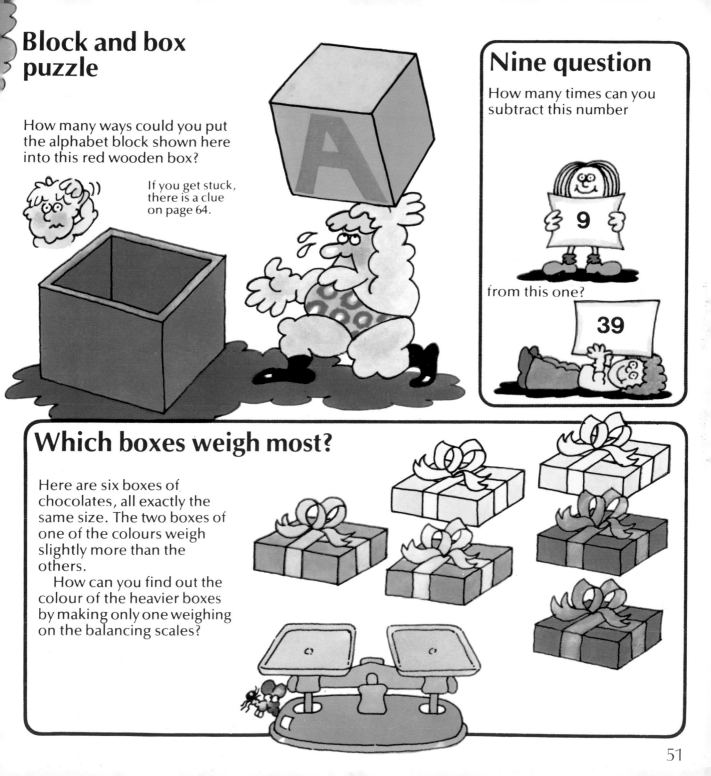

Nine question

How many times can you subtract this number

9

from this one?

39

Which boxes weigh most?

Here are six boxes of chocolates, all exactly the same size. The two boxes of one of the colours weigh slightly more than the others.

How can you find out the colour of the heavier boxes by making only one weighing on the balancing scales?

51

Value for money

Which of these packets of Marsbix should Marty Martian buy to get best value for money? (Remember, there are 50 Moons in 1 Dragon on Mars.)

NOW ONLY 50 Moons a packet

MARSBIX 400g

SPECIAL OFFER 2 PACKETS FOR 1 DRAGON 40 MOONS

300g 300g

Hole puzzle

If two people dig two holes in two days, how long does it take one person to dig one hole?

How big is the dinosaur?

This dinosaur's tail is twice as long as its body, which is half as long as its neck (to the end of its nose), which is 12m long. What does the dinosaur measure from nose to tail?

Number nature trail

There are lots of ways through Nature Walk Wood, but every time you pass something on the way you must collect points. What you have to do is find the path that takes you right through the wood with the smallest number of points.

Collect points as follows:

Add two points for each red thing you pass.

Add three points for each blue thing you pass.

Lose one point for each yellow thing you pass.

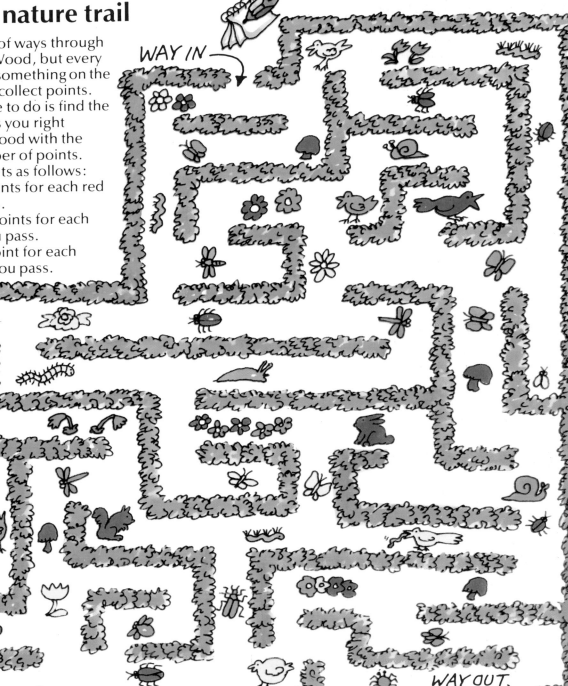

WAY IN

WAY OUT

53

Holiday puzzle

Jane's first purchase on her Spanish holiday was two cans of soft drink and an icecream. She paid 80 pesetas for them at a beach stall.

Later that day, she went back to the same stall and bought three cans of soft drink and two icecreams and was charged 130 pesetas.

How much does one can of soft drink cost in Spain?

80 PESETAS

130 PESETAS

? PESETAS

How far?

The ten children in this row are all standing the same distance apart. How far is it from Ann to Tony?

Still holding hands and staying the same distance apart, they move round to make a circle.

How far is it from Ann to Tony now?

←1½ metres→

54

How many children?

Two of the Smith children are in the football team and three are in the tennis team. What is the smallest possible number of children in the Smith family?

Stripey puzzle

Jim's Granny is knitting him a stripey scarf. Jim says the scarf must be 140cm long when it is finished and Granny says she will end with a red stripe. Each stripe measures 5cm.

How many blue stripes will there be in the finished scarf?

Millions of seconds

Have you any idea how long a million seconds is? Is it
a) 1½ years
b) 11½ days
or c) 46 hours?

Have a guess and then check the answer on page 63. You will probably be surprised.

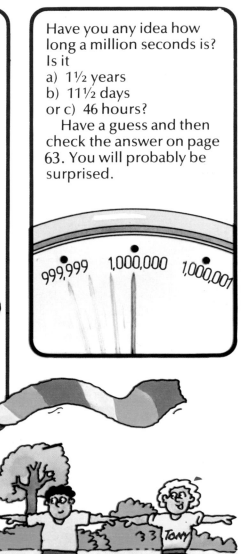

How many stones?

The stones for this gigantic pyramid have been dragged for hundreds of kilometres across the desert.

Can you work out how many blocks were needed to build the pyramid (including the one that is about to be hoisted into position)? The blocks are all the same size, by the way.

Lizzie's marble puzzle

Here's a bag of marbles Lizzie.

Hallo Billy. Would you like half of my marbles?

Yes please Lizzie.

Oh dear. I've lost half the marbles I had left after sharing with Billy. Now there are only six.

How many marbles did Lizzie have to start with?

Number jigsaw

See if you can fit the four pieces below into the spaces in the puzzle. When the puzzle is complete, the numbers must add up to 15 in every direction.

Egg puzzle

Sniffy and his two friends want an egg each every day. The three hens they have already lay three eggs in three days. How many more hens do they need?

Answers

Page 35

Can you do Martian maths?

 is 706.

is 558.

Marty's maths homework

a) ½ of 62 is 31 or 🙂 🙂 .
b) Melissa had 🙂 🙂 or 46 coins left.
c) It will take them 🙂 or 3 days to dig 3 holes.
d) Miranda is 3 or 🙂 .

Page 36

Ancient sum puzzle

The tablet reads:
13 + 271 + 5 + 487 = 776

Next number 1

The next number is 35.
The sequence is: 3 (+5) 8 (+7) 15 (+9) 24 (+11) 35.

Next number 2

The next number this time is 5.
The sequence is:
3 (−1) 2 (+2) 4 (−1) 3 (+2) 5.

What colour?

An odd number plus an even number is always an odd number, so the answer is red.

Page 37

How many chocolates?

127. Penny's brother has seven pockets, so he is asking for 1 + 2 + 4 + 8 + 16 + 32 + 64 = 127 chocolates.

Number boxes

Green box: All the numbers can be divided by 2, so any even number will do.

Pink box: All these numbers can be divided by 7, so 21, 28, 42, 56 or any other number you can divide by 7 will fit.

Cubes

All the smaller cubes, that is 8, will have some pattern on them.

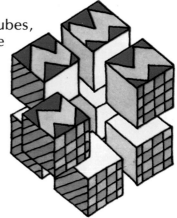

Page 38

Tennis game puzzle

They played six matches altogether:
Jo against Sue
Jo against Sam
Jo against Liz
Sue against Sam
Sue against Liz
Sam against Liz

Clare's cousins

Clare has 4 cousins. Here is her family tree to show you why.

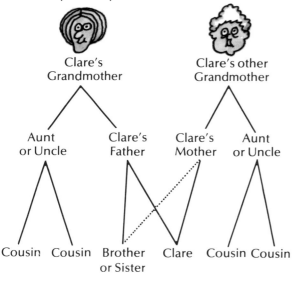

Page 39

Chocolate problem

There are 12 × 75g chocolate bars in a dozen.

Pie puzzle

There will be nine slices. Here is how to work it out:
6 equals ¾ of all slices except the big one, so 8 equals all the slices except the big one, and so there are 8 + 1 slices altogether.

How many squares?

There are 16 squares in the carpet.

Bicycle wheel sum

There are 16 spaces between the spokes. You can count them here.

Page 40

Which button?

Press the purple button (bottom right) to get out. This is what the completed square looks like:

16	2	3	13
5	11	10	8
9	7	6	12
4	14	15	1

Watch face sum

Picture D shows the correct answer.

Page 41

Magic numbers

Your answer is 7.

Lamp post puzzle

Dave has to walk 2½ times as far as Pete.

Quick question

The answer is 2. Here is how to work it out:
½ of 2 = 1.
1 ÷ ½ = 1 × 2/1 = 2.

Page 42

Martian cake

It cost Marty's mum 2 Dragons and 17 Moons to bake her cake.

Page 43

Model train problem

It takes two seconds for the train to pass completely through the tunnel. (It takes one second for the front to appear from the mouth of the tunnel and another second before the end of the train comes out.)

New numbers

 is 2749.

Washing day puzzle

45 minutes. (It takes exactly the same time to dry three shirts as it does to dry one.)

Page 44

Football shirt numbers

14 figure 1's are needed.

Here are all the numbers which contain a figure 1:
1, 10, 11, 12, 13, 14, 15, 16, 17, 18, 19, 21, 31.

The odd number

47 is the odd number. All the others can be divided by three.

Car parking puzzle

There are six different colour combinations. Here they are:

Page 45

How heavy is the cat?

The cat weighs 2,500g.
Here is how to work it out:
Top picture: cat + book = 7 jars
Bottom picture: 5 jars = 3 jars + book
Taking 2 jars from each side of scales:
                    2 jars = book
Top picture again, replacing book with jars:
                    cat + 2 jars = 7 jars
Taking 2 jars from each side:
                    cat = 5 jars
5 jars weigh 5 × 500g = 2,500g

Calendar counting

11. They all do except February.

How many people?

Answer a) – 30 million – is the nearest. (The distance round the Earth at the equator is

40,075km. An average person measures about 1½ metres, so roughly 26 million people would be needed to stretch round the Earth.)

Page 46

Garden path puzzle

The path is 100cm (1 metre) wide.
(If the snails start at the same time and go at the same speed, they must meet half way.)

Hungry bookworm

The bookworm must eat 6½cm to reach page number 1000. (Don't forget the worm is starting from the back of the book, so it must eat through one cover and 2,000 pages in order to reach page number 1000.)

Liquorice sticks

Spotty had four sticks left to share.

Page 47

Escaped zoo animals

Five animals were still free on the second day. Here is how to work it out:
20 animals escaped. On the first day 10 were captured. On the second day half of these (five) were captured, leaving five free.

How long is the railway track?

In real life the track would be 760 metres long.

Page 48

Mystery tour

Freddie's school went to the zoo. Here is the route they took to get there.

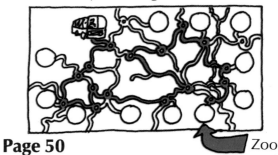

Page 50

Zoo

Park puzzle

There are 18 people in the park. You can see them here.

Page 51

Block and box puzzle

The block will fit into the box in 24 different ways.

Nine question

You can take 9 from 39 only once, because after you have taken 9 away you don't have 39 any more.

Which boxes weigh most?

Weigh a box of one colour, say a red one, against one of another colour, say a blue one. If they balance, then the third colour boxes must be the heavier ones. If they don't balance you will be able to see by which way the scale tips which colour is heavier.

Page 52

Value for money

The 50 Moon packet is better value. The special offer of two packets for 1 Dragon 40 Moons gives 600g for 90 Moons. At this rate, 400g costs 60 Moons. The separate packet gives 400g for 50 Moons, so it is cheaper.

How big is the dinosaur?

The dinosaur is 30m long.

NECK IS 12 M. LONG

BODY IS HALF NECK = 6 M.

TAIL IS TWICE BODY = 12 M.

Hole puzzle

It takes two days for one person to dig one hole.

Page 53

Number nature trail

This route scores least – 13 points.

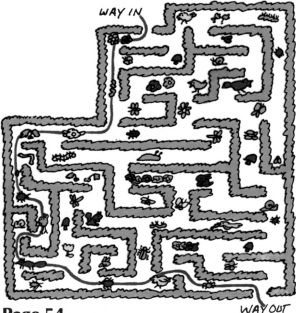

WAY IN

WAY OUT

Page 54

Holiday puzzle

One can of soft drink costs 30 pesetas. This is how to work it out:
1st picture: 2 cans + 1 ice = 80 pesetas.
2nd picture: 3 cans + 2 ices = 130 pesetas.
For an extra one can and one ice, Jane paid 50 pesetas more. This is 30 pesetas less than the cost of 2 cans + 1 ice. So 1 can costs 30.

How far?

When they are standing in a row, Ann and Tony are 13½m apart. When they move into a circle they are 1½m apart.

Page 55

How many children?

Three. Two of them could be in both teams.

Stripey puzzle

There will be nine blue stripes. Here is the finished scarf so you can count them.

Millions of seconds

A million seconds is about 11½ days (answer b)). If you have a calculator you can see for yourself.

Page 56

How many stones?
30 blocks are needed for this pyramid.
There are: 4 × 4 = 16 in the bottom layer.
             3 × 3 =   9 in the 2nd layer.
             2 × 2 =   4 in the 3rd layer.
             and 1 for the top.

Lizzie's marble puzzle

Lizzie started with 24 marbles.

Page 57

Number jigsaw puzzle

Here is the completed jigsaw.

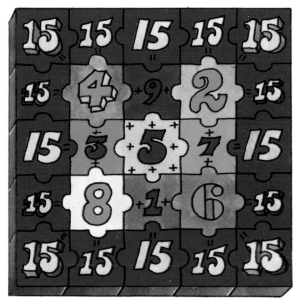

Egg puzzle

They need 6 more hens.
Here is how to work it out:
You know that in 3 days, 3 hens lay 3 eggs
so, in 1 day 3 hens lay 1 egg
but in 1 day Sniffy and friends need 3 eggs
so they need 3 times as many hens = 3 × 3
= 9 hens.
They already have 3, so they need 6 more.

Clues

Page 35
Can you do Martian maths?

Here are the Martian equivalents of Earth numbers 0 to 9:

Now see if you can do Marty's homework.

Page 36
Ancient sum puzzle

The sign: ⅃Ｌ on the tablet means +.
Can you work it out now?

Page 38
Tennis game puzzle

Take each person in turn and work out how many games she must play, then remember to take away the ones that are duplicated. For instance, count Jo plays Sue, but remember not to count Sue plays Jo because it is the same game.

Page 39
Pie puzzle

As the pie is round, the number of slices to the left of the big slice is the same as the number of slices to the right of it. Now see if you can work out how many slices there are.

Page 47
How long is the railway track?

A scale of 1:76 means that one unit of length on the model equals 76 of the same units in real life.

Page 51
Block and box puzzle

The block has six sides, so it can be turned to make the letter face in six separate directions.

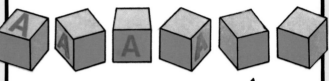

THE LETTER A IS ON THE BOTTOM
THE LETTER A IS ON THE FAR SIDE

In each of these positions, the letter can be four ways up, like this:

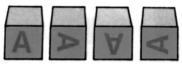

Now see if you can do the puzzle.

BRAIN PUZZLES

Contents

Hints on solving brain puzzles

The puzzles in this book are all brain teasers of various kinds. You will probably find some quite easy while others will make you think a bit.

When you are doing the puzzles, always read the question very carefully, bit by bit. Think about what each part means as you read through. You may need to read some of them several times to be quite sure of what you have to do.

If you can't work out the answer after a little thought, you may be on the wrong track. Try going back to the beginning again and thinking in a different direction. Don't give up too quickly – the answers are often quite obvious once you begin to look at the puzzle in the right way. Don't forget to be on the look out for trick questions either. Some of the puzzles are deliberately designed to mislead you and often sound much more difficult than they really are.

Some puzzles have this picture symbol next to them.

This means there is a clue at the end of the book. If you get stuck, look up the clue and it will give you some help without actually telling you the answer.

It will usually help to make notes as you work through a puzzle, so always have a pencil and some paper handy. When you see this picture symbol:

next to a puzzle, paper and pencil are essential.

You will find the answers to all the puzzles in this section on pages 90 to 95.

Who is right?

Marty Martian and his friends are out spotting wildlife and making notes about what they can see. The pages from their notebooks are shown on the right, below. Only one of them has correctly identified all the creatures in this picture.

Use this page from Marty's *Nature Guide to Mars* and work out who was right.

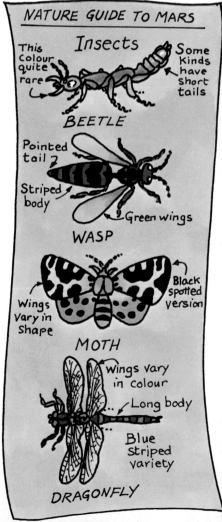

NATURE GUIDE TO MARS

Insects

This colour quite rare

Some kinds have short tails

BEETLE

Pointed tail

Striped body

Green wings

WASP

Wings vary in Shape

Black spotted version

MOTH

wings vary in colour

Long body

Blue striped variety

DRAGONFLY

MERVIN MARTIAN
3 Beetles
a wasp
one dragonfly
two moths
one unidentifiable creature

MANDY MARTIAN
3 things I can't identify
one wasp
one dragonfly
two moths

MAGGIE MARTIAN
One wasp
1 beetle
a dragonfly
2 moths
3 creatures which aren't in the book

MICKY MARTIAN
Two moths
2 beetles
2 I can't identify
2 dragonflies

67

Who typed the note?

Several days after the mysterious disappearance of a rich businessman's son, this letter was received through the post.

There were four people whom the police suspected of being involved with the case. Each of them had access to a typewriter which the police examined.

Can you work out who typed the letter from the following police information?

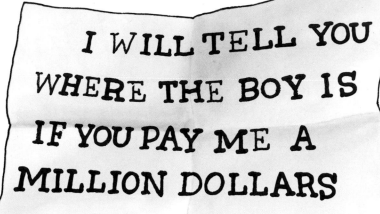

Whose party?

Joan is an only child. "I am going to a party," said Joan. "It is my mother's husband's daughter's birthday party." Whose party was it?

The typewriter in suspect 1's office types faintly on all letters but W and E.

The typewriter in suspect 2's shop types letters P and J out of line and letter E both faintly and out of line.

The typewriter in suspect 3's girl-friend's flat types the 23rd, fifth and seventh letters in the alphabet very faintly.

The typewriter in suspect 4's home types P and E faintly and every 10th letter out of line.

Sock puzzle

Jason had six blue socks and six green ones all mixed up in his drawer. One morning, still half-asleep, he pulled some socks out without looking.

What is the smallest number he had to pull out to be certain of getting two the same colour?

Which letter is missing?

Which of the spare placards below should the middle person in the line be holding?

How many children?

It is impossible to see small children when they are sitting in the deck-chairs on Sunny Sands beach.

See if you can work out the smallest possible number of occupied chairs from this information:

1) A boy is sitting on the right of a girl.
2) A girl is sitting on the right of a girl.
3) Two girls are sitting on the left of a boy.

Monster plant puzzle

Billy Bluefingers planted some Amazing New Monster Plant seeds in his Dad's greenhouse on Saturday.

"The plants will double in size each day," promised the packet . . . and they did. On the Thursday of the following week, the plants completely filled the greenhouse.

On which day was the greenhouse *half*-full of the plants?

Two train teaser

A local train, consisting of an engine and one very old carriage, is holding up the Express by stopping at every station. At last, it reaches a station with a siding.

The siding is very small, however. It can hold only one carriage *or* an engine, not both at once.

Can you work out what the trains should do in order to pass each other?

SIDING

LOCAL TRAIN

If you get stuck, look up the clue on page 96.

What does the machine do?

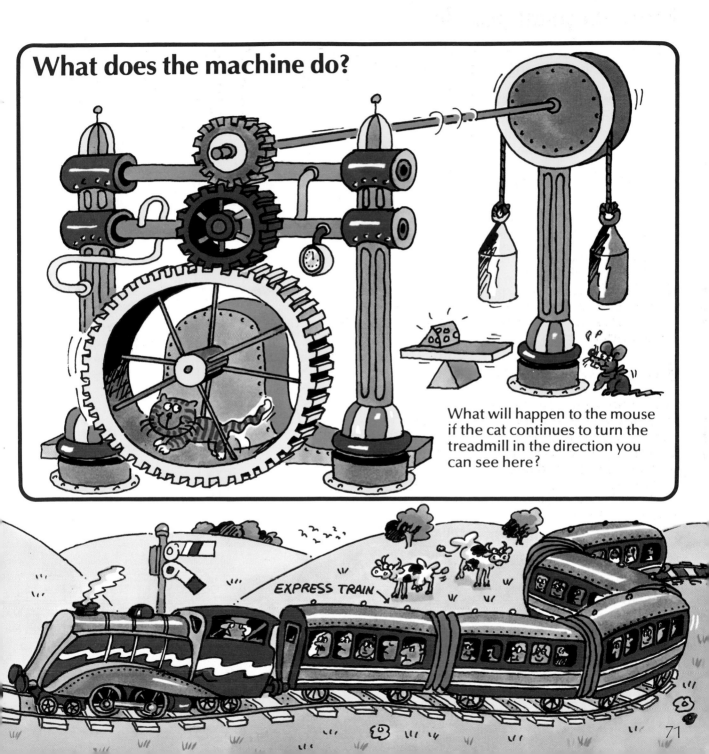

What will happen to the mouse if the cat continues to turn the treadmill in the direction you can see here?

EXPRESS TRAIN

71

Who lives where?

Can you work out who lives where from the following information?

1) Annie lives in a house with a green door. She passes all the other houses on her way to school.

2) Mick lives next door to a house with a green door and calls for Dan on his way to school.

3) Old Mrs Brown has a red front door. She has no children, but two children pass her house on the way to school.

4) Dan lives on the corner, next to the main road.

5) Ossie lives next door to Wendy and opposite Annie.

6) Jim's house has an odd number.

MAIN ROAD

SCHOOL

What day is it?

If yesterday's tomorrow was Thursday, what day is the day after tomorrow's yesterday?

How many fish?

Two fathers and three sons went fishing. They caught one fish each.

What is the smallest possible number of fish caught?

Tug-of-war puzzle

One day, the men working on the big Brick Road building site decided they could have a tug-of-war with their machines, using heavy steel cable.

See if you can work out who won their third contest, below.

In the **first contest,** two dumper trucks and a sand lorry beat a cement mixer.

In the **second contest,** one dumper truck and two sand lorries were beaten by a bulldozer.

The **third contest** was between a cement mixer and a sand lorry on one side and a bulldozer and a dumper truck on the other.

Cocoa mug puzzle

Wesley and the gang were drinking their bed-time cocoa round the camp fire and feeling a bit bored. Then Lenny had an idea.

"Look!" he said, "I've made a pyramid shape on the ground with our mugs. I bet none of you can reverse the pyramid by moving only three mugs."

After about fifteen minutes, Wesley had the answer. Can you work it out too (and more quickly)?

Who did it?

"Who did it?" spluttered Old Mrs Grumpy, when she found her window was broken.

I didn't.

Bob did.

Rocky is lying.

CASSIE

ROCKY

BOB

Only one of them is telling the truth; the other two are lying. Who broke the window?

If you get stuck, look at the clue on page 96.

74

Six oranges

There are six oranges in this bag. How can you give these six children an orange each and still have one left in the bag?

How many cakes?

How many cakes do you think there should be on the plate in the third picture below?

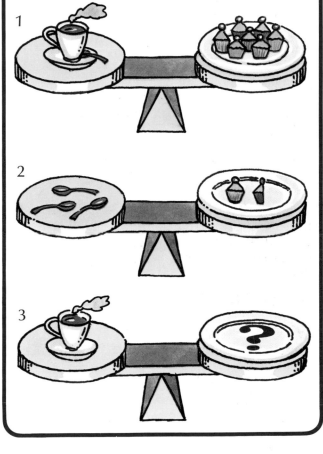

1

2

3

How many cubes?

Which of these shapes, if folded along the dotted lines, could be made into cubes?

This is what a cube looks like.

1

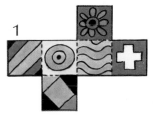

2

3

4

Spy message

This message, which is, of course, in code, was sent to a member of an international spy ring. Shortly after it arrived, his telephone rang and a muffled voice whispered, "14 is N".

The spy was then able to decode the message and read it. Can you?

If you get stuck, look at the clue on page 96.

4.15./14.15.20./20.18.21.19.20./

2.18.15.23.14./8.5./9.19./

1./4.15.21.2.12.5./

1.7.5.14.20.

A. Wellwisher

Water puzzle

Sarah's cake recipe said she needed 100ml of water. She found two jugs in the kitchen. One held exactly 500ml, the other exactly 400ml.

After some thought, she realized she could measure 100ml using just these two jugs.

Can you work out how she did it?

How high is the wall?

When this wall is finished it will be ten bricks high. Here are the measurements of the bricks being used:

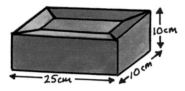

The builder is putting a layer of cement 2cm deep between each row of bricks. How high will the wall be when it is finished?

Toy brick puzzle

Sam's elder sister has set him this problem. Sam is only four, however, and he can't do it. See if you can help him.

Ten of Sam's bricks are laid out on the floor as shown on the right.

Sam has to move (not remove) just one brick in order to turn the pattern into a regular cross with six bricks in each row.

If you get stuck, look at the clue on page 96.

Separate the people

Can you see where four new straight walls should be built in this office to give each person his or her own room?

There is one catch – the new walls must make a square.

77

The Seven O'Clock Club

Poppy, Alice, Dave and Tim all belong to the Seven O'Clock Club. See if you can work out who is likely to be at the club each night.

Seven O'Clock Club

Monday and Wednesday: Table Tennis
Tuesday: Darts
Thursday: Folk Night

Friday: Jazz night
Saturday: Rock night
Sunday: closed

Put the apples in the bags

Imagine you have nine apples and four large paper bags. How can you put an odd number of apples into each bag? You are not allowed to cut up any of the apples or tear the bags.

Poppy likes all kinds of music, but dislikes darts and table tennis. She goes out on Wednesdays and Saturdays.

Alice is free to go out on any night except Thursdays. She does not like darts, but often plays table tennis. She also likes all kinds of music.

Tim is club table tennis champion. He likes darts and folk music, but not rock or jazz. He goes out on Mondays, Wednesdays and Saturdays.

Dave hates table tennis and the only music he likes is jazz. He often has a game of darts and his nights out are on Mondays, Tuesdays and Fridays.

Dead-end puzzle

Workmen have accidentally trapped these four people in a narrow alley. The people in red hats could squeeze past the roadworks if they could get past the people in blue hats. The doorway is big enough for just one person (red hat or blue hat) to stand in at a time.

Can you work out how the two people in red hats can get out of the alley before the workmen remove the blockage? (The diagram at the bottom of the page should help you.)

How many creepy-crawlies?

If these three creatures are creepy-crawlies,

but the three creatures below are not creepy-crawlies,

then which of these are creepy-crawlies?

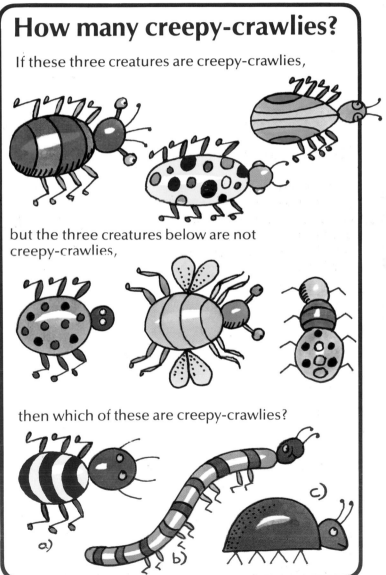

Brain maze

The Martian Government Building is controlled by an enormous computer – "The Brain". The Brain has electronic eyes, ears and feeling and smelling devices dotted around the building with which it can detect strangers.

Can Marty and his friend sneak into the building and give Marty's Dad his lunch box without The Brain noticing?

FEELING DEVICE

THE BRAIN

T.V. SCREENS 1 AND 2

T.V. CAMERA No. 2

MARTY'S DAD'S OFFICE

ELECTRONIC LISTENING DEVICE

GUARD

EMERGENCY STAIRS

LIFT ONLY OPERATED BY KNOWN FINGERS

LIFT CAN BE OPERATED BY ANYONE

ELECTRONIC EYE

PRESSURE SENSITIVE FLOOR WHICH RECOGNIZES STRANGERS

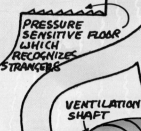

MEETING OF MARTIAN ELDERS

VENTILATION SHAFT

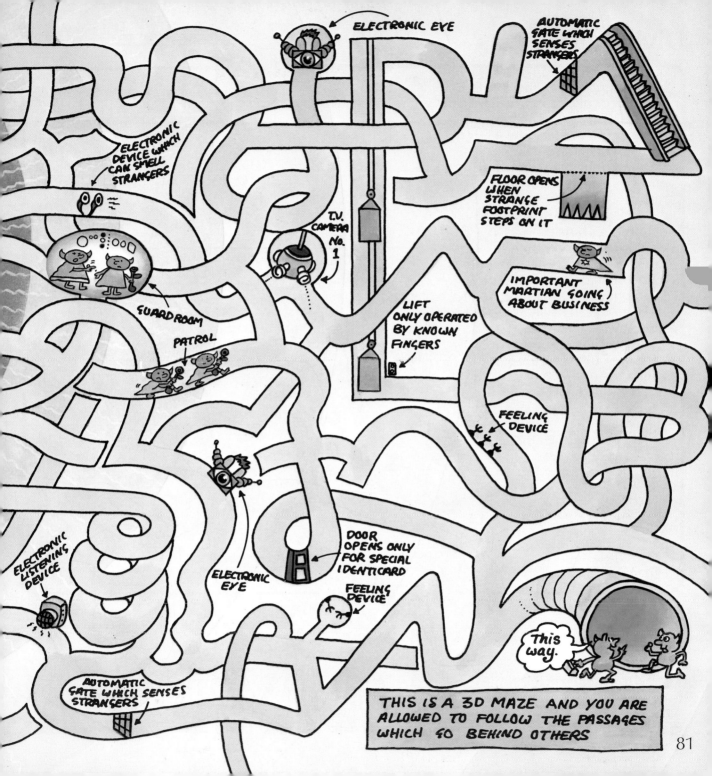

Divide up the cats

When Aunt Chloe died, she left her entire collection of valuable Siamese cats to her nieces and nephew. Her eldest niece, Emily, was to have half; nephew Sebastian, one-third; and great niece Jane, one-ninth.

Uncle Albert (a keen Siamese cat breeder himself) was appointed to carry out the terms of the will. This was quite a problem for him, for Aunt Chloe had left 17 cats. None of the cats was to be shared, sold, given away or killed.

Uncle Albert found a way of carrying out the terms of the will in the end. Can you work out how he did it?

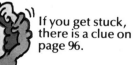
If you get stuck, there is a clue on page 96.

Who is wrong?

One of the people in this row is holding one of his flags in the wrong position. Can you work out who it is?

1 2 3 4 5 6

School journey puzzle

Whizzer, Lightning and Snail all left their homes in different parts of the town at 8.00 a.m. Whizzer cycled at an average speed of 20kph. Snail walked at 5kph. Lightning travelled in his father's car which averaged 60kph.

They all arrived at the school gates at the same time. Whose journey took the longest?

How heavy is the chocolate bar?

One Super Giant Size Nut-filled Chocolate Bar balances with a ¼kg weight and three-quarters of a Super Giant Size Nut-filled Chocolate Bar. How much does half a Super Giant Size Nut-filled Chocolate Bar weigh?

Which colour?

What colour was the robbers' getaway car? Read this story and see if you can work it out.

The police already knew the robbers' car was either red or blue. Luckily Charlie saw the robbery and was able to tell them which it was.

Charlie's brother later told some friends what had happened.
 "Charlie said the car was blue," he said.

The problem is that one of the brothers always tells the truth, but we don't know which. The other always tells lies.

Mend the broken necklace

Can you mend this necklace by working out in which order the spare beads should be threaded?

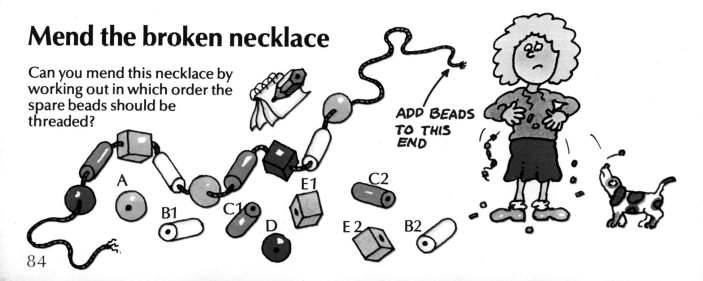

ADD BEADS TO THIS END

A
B1
C1
D
E1
C2
E2
B2

Cat and mouse puzzle

Look at this picture. Can the mouse reach its hole before the cat can catch it?

CAT IS 40 METRES FROM MOUSE

MOUSE IS 20 METRES FROM HOLE

On your marks..

MOUSE HOLE

CAT RUNS AT 20 METRES A SECOND

MOUSE RUNS AT 10 METRES A SECOND

The new princedom

King Krust told his son, Krum, he could have as much land as he liked for his princedom as long as he followed these rules:
1) The border must consist of just three straight lines.
2) The third line must return to the point where the first one started from.
3) The border must touch each of the four city pictures shown on this map.

Can you work out where Prince Krum drew his three border lines?

PRINCETON

KING CITY

ROYAL CITY

QUEEN CITY

Space buggy puzzle

Imagine you are the captain of a space mission to a distant planet. Your job is to bring back to Earth examples of any strange forms of life, and you have just found the three creatures shown in this picture.

You have room for only one passenger at a time in your space buggy.

I attack anything green.

I am friendly.

How can you carry all three creatures back to your space station without them destroying each other?

I eat robots.

If you get stuck, look up the clue on page 96.

Bicycle race puzzle

"I will buy an enormous cream cake for the one whose bike comes second in a race to the end of the street," said Eddy's Mum as she left for the shops.

Eddy and his friend both love cakes, so they started straight away. But they went slower and slower until, finally, they both refused to go any further in case they came first.

They argued for a while, then finally agreed that there was only one way of continuing the race so that one of them could win the cake.

Can you work out what they decided to do?

If you get stuck, look at the clue on page 96.

Cut the cake

Can you cut this cake into eight equal size pieces using only three cuts of the knife?

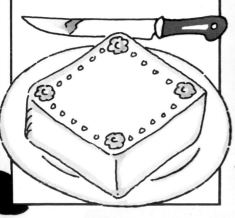

Fence the goats in

Three unfriendly goats need putting in separate pens to stop them fighting. There are seven pieces of fencing, all the same length.

Where would you position the fences to make pens for the goats?

You may find it easier to work this out by using seven matchsticks for the fences.

87

Bridge-crossing puzzle

This deep canyon is not far from Marty Martian's home on Mars. Two flat topped hills in the middle of the canyon are linked to the edges with rope bridges, as you can see in the picture.

Marty and his friends know a way of crossing every bridge once without retracing their steps. (They can start and finish where they like, but cannot climb down into the canyon.)

See if you can work out the route they take.

How old are they?

HARRY

I'm twice as old as you.

But in five years' time I shall be as old as you are now.

HELEN

Luxury yacht puzzle

See if you can work out the answer to this problem which Herb E. Dollar, the famous millionaire, set the guests on his luxury yacht. (The yacht was moored in the harbour at the time.)

The metal ladder hanging from the side of the yacht has eight rungs set ⅓ metre apart. At low tide, the water comes up as far as the fourth rung. As the tide comes in, the height of the water in the harbour increases at the rate of ⅓ metre an hour. How long will it take for the water to reach the top rung of the ladder?

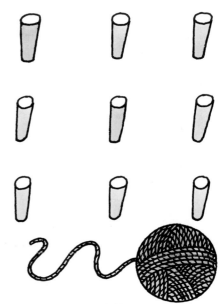

String and peg puzzle

Here are nine pegs, fixed firmly into the ground, and a big ball of string.

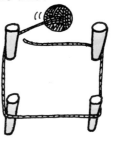

How many different squares could you make by winding the string round sets of four pegs, like this?

Answers

Page 67

Who is right?

Maggie Martian has identified all the creatures correctly. Here you can see what they all are.

Page 68

Who typed the note?

Suspect 3 did it.

Whose party?

It was Joan's party.

Page 69

Sock puzzle

Jason had to pull three socks out of the drawer to be sure of getting a pair. Here is how he worked it out:

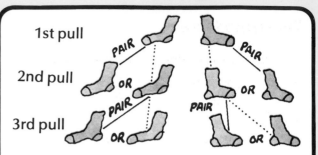

Whatever happens, he has a pair of one or other colour by the third pull.

Which letter is missing?

Placard 2: letter K.
(Three letters are missed out between each one.)

How many children?

Three. Here they are:

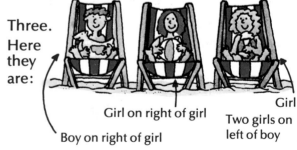

Girl on right of girl

Girl

Two girls on left of boy

Boy on right of girl

("Left" and "right" are used here as if you were looking from the back, as you were in the puzzle picture on page 5.)

Page 70

Monster plant puzzle

The greenhouse was half-full on Wednesday. (The plants double in size each day, so the day on which the greenhouse is half-full is the day before it is full.)

Two train teaser

Local train backs into siding and unhooks carriage.

Engine moves off up track, well clear of the station.

Express train moves up past siding, backs so that end carriage can hook onto spare carriage.

Express moves forward pulling spare carriage out of siding with it and then backs off down track again.

Local train engine backs into siding.

Express train unhooks local carriage, leaves it on track and moves up line beyond station.

Local engine comes out siding and backs down track to pick up its carriage.

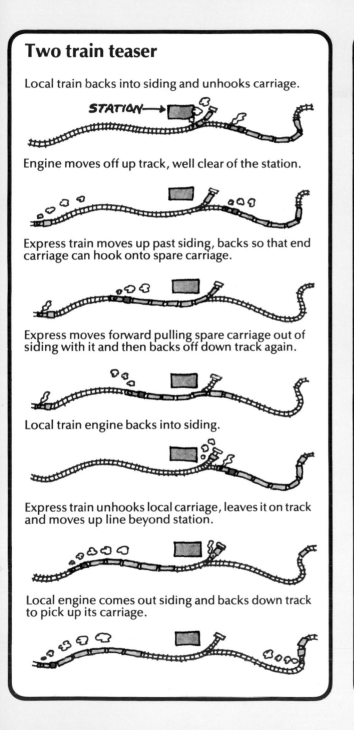

STATION →

Page 71

What does the machine do?

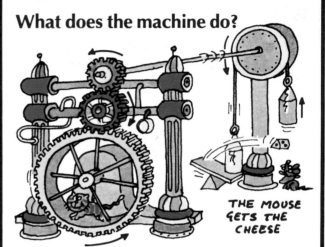

THE MOUSE GETS THE CHEESE

Page 72

Who lives where?

Here are the house numbers and the names of their occupants:

1	Jim	5	Wendy
2	Dan	6	Old Mrs Brown
3	Mick	7	Ossie
4	Judy	8	Annie

Page 73

What day is it?

Friday.

How many fish?

Three. The two fathers are also sons, so the smallest number of fishermen is three, and they each caught a fish.

Tug-of-war puzzle

The bulldozer and dumper truck won the third contest.

Page 74

Cocoa mug puzzle

Move the mugs like this to reverse the pyramid:

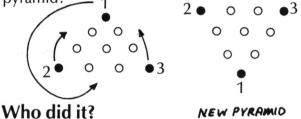

NEW PYRAMID

Who did it?

Cassie did.

Page 75

Six oranges

Take five oranges out of the bag and give one to each of five of the children. Then give the sixth child the bag containing the orange that is left.

How many cakes?

There should be 6½ cakes on the third plate.

How many cubes?

Pictures 1 and 4 can be folded up to make cubes. The other two cannot.

Page 76

Spy message

The message reads: "Do not trust Brown. He is a double agent."
(The code is 1 = A, 2 = B, 3 = C, and so on.)

Water puzzle

Fill the 500ml jug right to the top from the tap. Now fill the 400ml jug to the top from the 500ml jug. The 500ml jug has exactly 100ml left in it.

Page 77

Toy brick puzzle

Move the top brick and put it on top of the centre one. You now have six bricks in each row and a cross with equal length arms.

How high is the wall?

118cm (or 1 metre 18cm).

Separate the people

Here are the four new walls:

Page 78

The Seven O'Clock Club

Monday: Alice and Tim
Tuesday: Dave
Wednesday: Alice and Tim
Thursday: No-one
Friday: Alice and Dave
Saturday: Poppy and Alice
Sunday: No-one

Put the apples in the bags

Put three apples into each of three bags. Then put these three bags into the fourth bag.

Page 79

How many creepy-crawlies?

Creature b) is a creepy-crawly. The other two are not.
(Creepy-crawlies have eight legs, green eyes and stripes or spots on their bodies. Their bodies are made up of only one part.)

Dead-end puzzle

These pictures show how the people in red hats manage to get out.

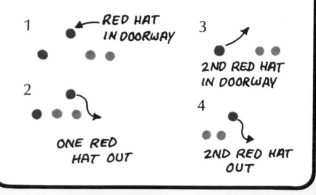

Page 80   Brain maze   Here is the route Marty and his friend must take to reach Marty's Dad's office safely.

Page 82

Divide up the cats

Uncle Albert added one of his own cats, making 18 in all. He then gave half (9) to Emily, one-third (6) to Sebastian and one-ninth (2) to Jane. This left one over, so he kept it to replace the one he had added.

Who is wrong?

Person 4 is wrong. He should be holding the flag in his left hand like this:

Page 83

School journey puzzle

No-one's. They all left home at the same time and arrived at the same time.

How heavy is the chocolate bar?

Half a Super Giant-Size Nut-filled Chocolate Bar weighs ½kg.

Page 84

Which colour?

The car was red. Work it out like this:
If Charlie's brother is lying, then Charlie must have said the car was *red*. In this case, Charlie is the one who is telling the truth, so the car was red.

If Charlie's brother is telling the truth, then Charlie did say the car was blue. In this case, though, Charlie is the liar, so really the car was red.

Mend the broken necklace

The spare beads should be threaded in this order:

Page 85

Cat and mouse puzzle

Yes. The mouse can reach its hole before the cat can catch it.

The new princedom

Here are Prince Krum's borders:

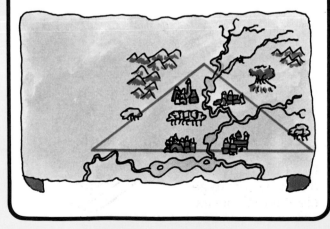

Page 86

Space buggy puzzle

Here are the trips you must make in the space buggy:

Red stripey and Robot — Trip 1 / Green monster →

Red stripey and Robot ← Trip 2 / empty seat — Green monster

Red stripey — Trip 3 / Robot → Green monster

Red stripey ← Trip 4 / Green monster — Robot

Green monster — Trip 5 / Red stripey → Robot

Green monster ← Trip 6 / empty seat — Robot and Red stripey

— Trip 7 / Green monster → Robot and Red stripey

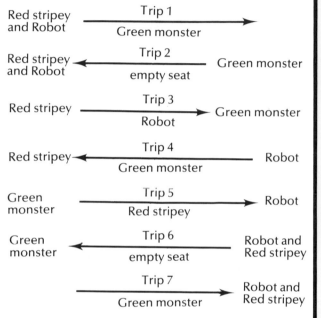

Page 87

Bicycle race puzzle

Eddy and his friend swopped bikes and then rode as fast as they could to try and come first on the other one's bike. (The one whose *bike* came second got the cake.)

Cut the cake

Here is where to make the three cuts to get eight equal pieces:

Fence the goats in

The seven pieces of fencing should be positioned like this:

Page 88

Bridge-crossing puzzle

This is the route Marty and his friends take across the canyon bridges.

How old are they?

Helen is 5. Harry is 10.

Page 89

Luxury yacht puzzle

The water will never reach the top rung of the ladder (unless the boat sinks). The ship with the ladder attached rises with the tide and the water stays at the same level in relation to it.

String and peg puzzle

You can make six squares. Here they are:

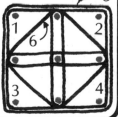

Clues

Page 70

Two train teaser

Try backing the local train into the siding, unhooking the carriage and leaving it there. You will need to move both trains backwards and forwards along the track several times.

Page 74

Who did it?

Remember only one of them is telling the truth. Try each one in turn and see if it is possible for he or she to be telling the truth while the other two are lying.

Page 76

Spy message

A second phone call came later and the same muffled voice whispered, ". . . and 1 is A".

Page 77

Toy brick puzzle

You are allowed to pile one brick on top of another. By the way, a regular cross has equal length arms like this:

Page 82

Divide up the cats

Notice that Uncle Albert breeds Siamese cats himself. What would happen if he added one of his own to Aunt Chloe's?

Page 86

Space buggy puzzle

Take the green monster with you on your first trip back to the space station. You will then need to make three more trips in each direction. You won't always have an empty seat on your trips back to the place where the space creatures were found.

Page 87

Bicycle race

Read the first sentence of this puzzle again very carefully and notice that Eddy's Mum promises the cake to the one whose *bike* comes second. Now think again.

This edition published 1993.
First published in 1980 by Usborne Publishing Ltd, Usborne House, 83-85 Saffron Hill, London EC1N 8RT.
Copyright © 1993, 1980 Usborne Publishing Ltd.

The name Usborne and the device USBORNE are Trade Marks of Usborne Publishing Ltd.

Printed in Belgium.